Treasury

Peppa Pig™: Peppa's School Day (978-0-545-92547-1)
© Astley Baker Davies Ltd/Entertainment One UK Ltd 2003.
Peppa Pig™: Peppa Visits the Aquarium (978-1-338-05417-0)
© Astley Baker Davies Ltd/Entertainment One UK Ltd 2003.
Peppa Pig™: Daddy Pig's Old Chair (978-1-338-18305-4)
© Astley Baker Davies Ltd/Entertainment One UK Ltd 2003.
Peppa Pig™: Recycling Fun! (978-1-338-18326-9)
© Astley Baker Davies Ltd/Entertainment One UK Ltd 2003.
Peppa Pig™: Peppa Goes Swimming (978-0-545-83491-9)
© Astley Baker Davies Ltd/Entertainment One UK Ltd 2003.
Peppa Pig™: Class Trip (978-0-545-52402-5)
© Astley Baker Davies Ltd/Entertainment One UK Ltd 2003.

 ISBN 978-1-338-18684-0

10 9 8 7 6 5 4 3 2   17 18 19 20 21

Printed in Malaysia
First printing 2017

108

Contents

Peppa's School Day

Peppa Visits the Aquarium

Daddy Pig's Old Chair

Recycling Fun!

Class Trip

Peppa Goes Swimming

Peppa's School Day

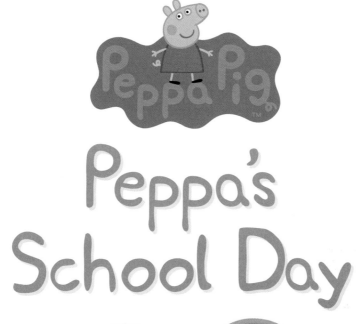

Peppa's
School Day

Adapted by Meredith Rusu

In this story, you will see:

Peppa

Suzy Sheep

slide

Madame Gazelle

Emily Elephant

building blocks

Peppa is going to school today.

All of her friends are there!

"Today we have a new
student," says Madame Gazelle.
"This is Emily Elephant."

Emily is shy.
She does not know what to say.

Everyone is excited to meet
Emily!
"Can I show Emily how we do
show-and-tell?" Peppa asks.

"Of course," says Madame
Gazelle.
Peppa tells the class about
her teddy bear.

Next, it is free time.

"What would you like to do today?" Peppa asks Emily.

There is painting, clay, or building blocks.

Emily chooses building blocks!

Peppa shows Emily how to stack the blocks.

"You put one on top of another," says Peppa.

"Like this?" asks Emily.
"Wow!" say the children.

Emily Elephant is good at
stacking blocks!

Next, it is playtime!
"Come on, Emily," shouts
Peppa.

"At playtime, we go outside!"
says Candy Cat.

All the children run outside.

First, they go down the slide.

Wheeeee!

Then they play a game.
"Who is the loudest?" asks
Peppa. *Snort!*

Oink!
Snort!

They all make loud sounds.
What a lot of noise!

"Emily, you try," says Peppa.
Emily makes a noise like a
trumpet.

She is the loudest of all!

"Can you spin the hula hoop?" Suzy Sheep asks Emily.

Emily can spin the hula hoop.
She is good at lots of things!

But there is still one game left to play.

"My favorite game is jumping in muddy puddles," says Peppa. "That is my favorite game, too!" shouts Emily.

Peppa and Emily are so happy
they are friends.
What a nice day at school!

Peppa Visits the Aquarium

Peppa Visits the Aquarium

Adapted by Meredith Rusu

In this story, you will see:

Peppa

George

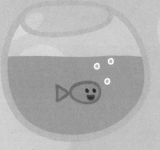

Goldie

Miss Rabbit

Candy Cat

aquarium

Every morning, Peppa gives
Goldie, her pet fish, breakfast.

"Time to eat!" she says.

Oh, dear.
Goldie is not eating.

"What is wrong with Goldie?"
Peppa asks.

"She looks a bit sad," says
Mummy Pig.

"I think she is lonely," says Peppa. "She doesn't have any fish friends."

"Maybe Goldie could visit the aquarium," says Daddy Pig.

"What is the aquarium?"
Peppa asks.

"It is a place with lots of fish," says Daddy Pig.

"Oh, goodie!" cries Peppa.
"We can find a friend for
Goldie there. Let's go!"

Peppa and her family drive to
the aquarium.
Beep, beep!

Miss Rabbit sells them tickets.

"The fish can go in for free!" she says. "Enjoy your visit!"

The first room has many little fish.
"Could one of these fish be Goldie's new friend?" asks Daddy Pig.

Peppa's friend, Candy Cat, is in the next room with her family.

"Hello, Candy!" says Peppa.
"We are finding a friend for
Goldie."

The fish in this room look like little dinosaurs.

"Dine-saw!" says George.

"These aren't dinosaurs," says Candy. "They are called sea horses."

"Could a sea horse be Goldie's friend?" Candy asks.

"No," says Peppa. "They are too dinosaur-y."

Everyone goes to the next room.

The tank in here has a very strange fish.

"Wow!" says Daddy Pig. "This fish looks like a big eye!"

It is a big eye . . . on a very
BIG fish!
"Maybe this one could be
Goldie's new friend!" says
Mummy Pig.

"No," says Peppa. "It is TOO big!"
Glub, glub!

There is only one room left
to visit.
    But there are no fish in this
tank. There is only green slime.

Oh! And Miss Rabbit is in the tank, too.
She is cleaning it.

The last stop is the café.
"We did not find a friend for
Goldie," Peppa says sadly.
Then, Peppa notices a bowl on
the counter.

"What is that?" Peppa asks.
"This is my pet goldfish,
Ginger," says Miss Rabbit.

Goldie likes Ginger.
Ginger likes Goldie.

"Goldie can visit Ginger any time she wants," says Miss Rabbit.

Glub, glub!
Hee, hee!
Goldie has made a friend at the aquarium after all.

Daddy Pig's
Old Chair

Daddy Pig's Old Chair

Adapted by Ellen Philpott

In this story, you will see:

chair

Peppa

Madame Gazelle

Daddy Pig

Mummy Pig

rummage sale

"We have to buy
a new school roof,"
says Madame Gazelle.
"We will have a rummage
sale to make money."

Peppa gives her toys to the
rummage sale, to make money.

"I will give this toy, too,"
says Peppa.

"You can give this old chair,
Daddy," says Peppa.

"No. This is a very good chair,"
says Daddy Pig.

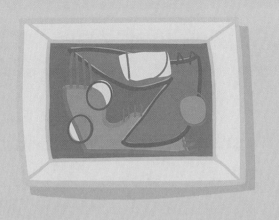

Peppa gives all the toys
to Madame Gazelle.

"You can have this old chair, too,"
says Mummy Pig.

Peppa, Mummy Pig, and Daddy Pig go to the rummage sale. Peppa's friends go, too.

Daddy's chair is at the rummage sale. It looks very old.

Peppa looks at all the toys with her friends. Her old toy looks very good.

"I will buy my old toy back," says Peppa.

All her friends buy their old toys back, too.

"I will buy this chair," says Daddy. "It will look good with the old one."

"No. It IS the old one!"
says Mummy Pig.

"Oh. It was a lot of money," says
Daddy Pig.

"Good," says Madame Gazelle.
"We have made
a lot of money. We can
buy a new school roof!"

Peppa is glad buying her toy back helped her school. And Daddy Pig is glad he has his chair back!

Peppa Pig

Recycling Fun!

Recycling Fun!

Adapted by Lorraine Horsley

In this story, you will see:

Mummy Pig

Peppa

George

car

Daddy Pig

truck

Mr. Bull

newspapers

bottles

cans

Miss Rabbit

Mr. Bull is collecting trash.

Mr. Bull puts the trash in the back of his truck.

Peppa, George, and Mummy Pig are collecting trash, too.

They collect bottles, cans, and newspapers.

"We can recycle much of this trash," says Mummy Pig.

They put the trash
in the car.

Mummy Pig has
all the bottles.

Peppa has all the cans.

George has all the newspapers.

Miss Rabbit is recycling
trash, too. She is
recycling cars.

Daddy Pig recycles the bottles.

Mummy Pig and Peppa recycle the cans.

"I like this!" Peppa says.

George recycles the
newspapers.

Oh no! Miss Rabbit is recycling
Daddy Pig's car!

"Stop!" says Daddy Pig. "Stop!
That is not recycling! That is
our car!"

"Oh," says Miss Rabbit.
"I like recycling too much!"

"Our car is not trash," says
Daddy Pig.

"No," says Peppa.
"We like our car!"

"And now we like to recycle, too!"
Peppa says. *Hee, hee! Snort!*

Class Trip

Adapted by Ellen Philpott

In this story, you will see:

Peppa

Danny Dog

ducks

bus

mountain

Peppa and her friends are going on a school trip.

"Is everyone here?" asks Madame Gazelle.

"Yes," they say.

Everyone loves school trips.

"Where are we going for our trip?" asks Peppa.

"We are going to the mountains," says Madame Gazelle.

"Hooray!" everyone cheers.

The bus is going to the top of a big mountain. It is very high up.

"Come on, bus!" says Peppa.

Up, up, up they go.

The bus gets to the top and everyone gets out.

"Come and look at the big mountains," says Madame Gazelle.

Peppa looks at the mountains. She is very high up.

"Wow," she says.

Everyone hears, "Wow, wow, wow."

"What was that?" asks Peppa.

"That was an echo", says Madame Gazelle. "It is what you hear when you call out, up in the mountains."

"Come on, everyone," says Peppa.
"We can all make an echo."

The children call out, "Wow."
Then they hear, "Wow, wow, wow."

Wow Wow Wow

Snort!   Baaa!

Woof!

"Come on, children," says
Madame Gazelle. "It is time for
our picnic."

"Hooray!" everyone cheers.

"Where are the ducks?" asks Peppa. "They love it when we have picnics, too."

Peppa and her friends look out for the ducks.

Quack! Quack! Quack! Here come the ducks!
"Hello! Would you like some bread?"
Peppa asks them.

The ducks are very lucky today. The kids brought plenty of extra bread to feed them!

"Come here, ducks," says Madame Gazelle.

"Yes, join our picnic, ducks," says Peppa.

The ducks have a big picnic, too.

It is time to go back to school. The children get on the bus. Then they sing a song as they go back down the mountain.

Everyone loves school bus trips!

Peppa Goes Swimming

Peppa Goes Swimming

In this story, you will see:

 Peppa

George

 Daddy Pig

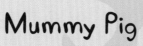

Mummy Pig

Rebecca Rabbit

watering can

It is a warm summer day.

Peppa and her family are at the
swimming pool.

"Peppa, George, let Daddy put on your swimming armbands," says Mummy Pig.

Today is George's first time at the
pool. He's scared of getting in the
water.

"Why don't you put just one foot in?"
asks Daddy Pig.

"Maybe George should try both feet
at the same time," says Mummy Pig.

"Grunt! Hee! Hee! Snort!" shouts George happily.

"Ho! Ho! Well done, George!" snorts Daddy Pig.

Rebecca Rabbit, her brother, Richard, and their mother arrive at the pool, too.

"Richard, hold on to this float. You can practice kicking your legs," says Mrs. Rabbit.

"George, would you like to try kicking your legs, too?" asks Mummy Pig.

"Hee! Hee! Snort!" giggles George.

"Big children are good at swimming," says Peppa. "When George and Richard are older, they will be able to swim like us. Won't they, Rebecca?"

"Yes!" says Rebecca. She watches the boys kick and splash.

Peppa and Rebecca race each other up and down the pool with their swimming armbands on.

They have lots of fun swimming and splashing in the water!

Oops! Richard dropped his toy watering can into the pool.

"Mummy! Wah!" cries Richard.

"Sorry, Richard, I can't reach it. It's too far down," says Mrs. Rabbit.

Luckily, Daddy Pig is an excellent swimmer. He takes off his glasses and dives down to get Richard's watering can.

"Ho! Ho! There you go!" Daddy Pig snorts.

"Squeak, squeak!" says Richard.

"Well done, Daddy Pig!" says Mummy Pig.

"Thank you, Daddy Pig," says Mrs. Rabbit.

Oh, dear! Richard is so happy to have his watering can back that he splashes Daddy Pig with water!

"Hee! Hee! Hee!" George laughs.

What a silly little piggy and rabbit!

Everyone had fun swimming at the pool!